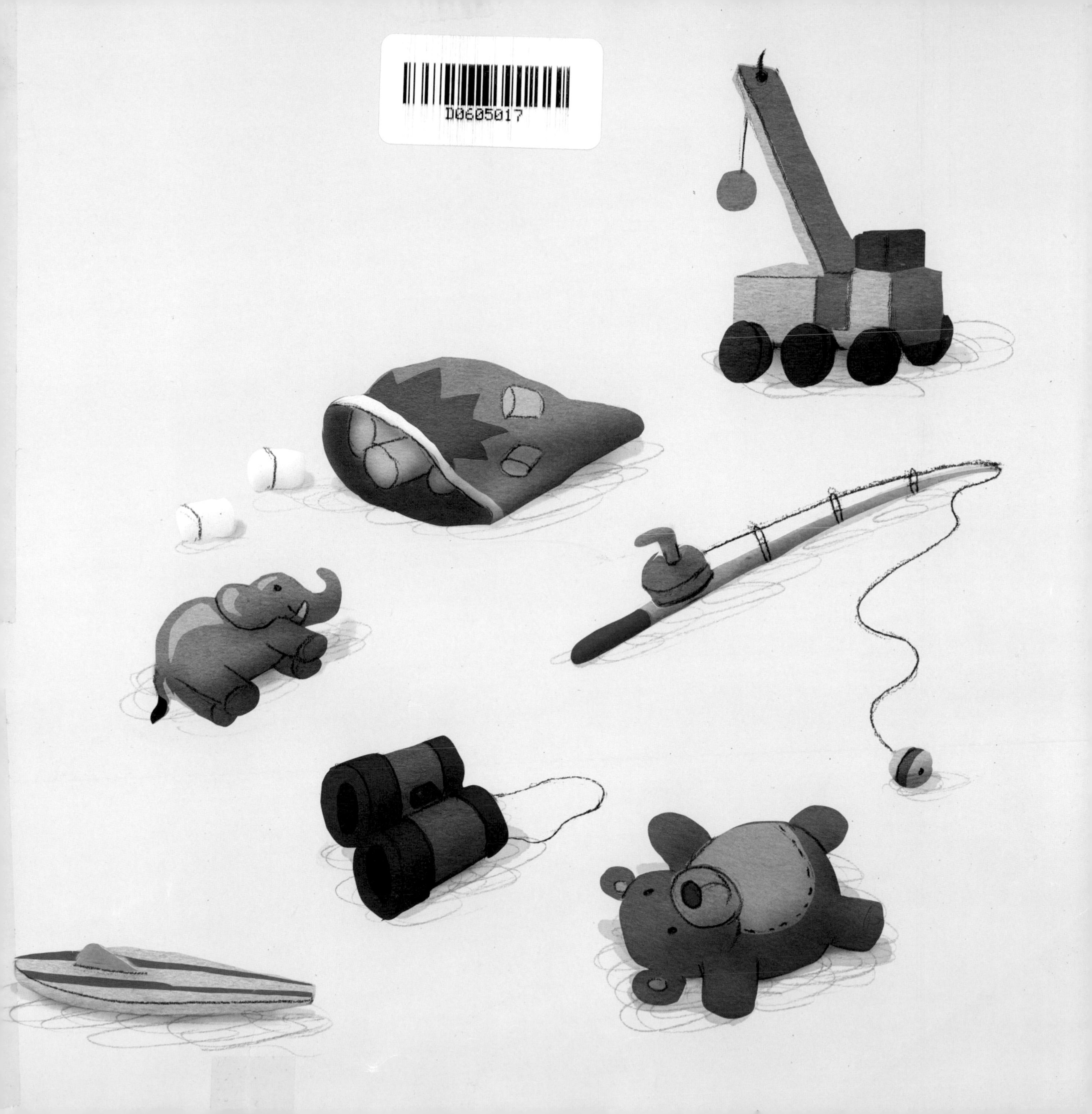

For my sons, Tyler and Benjamin —L.R.

For my grandfather, who told my dad to follow his dreams.
And for my dad, who taught me to follow mine.
—J.M.

 Published in the United States by Doubleday, an imprint of Random House Children's Books, a division of Penguin Random House LLC, New York.
Doubleday and the colophon are registered trademarks of Penguin Random House LLC.

Visit us on the Web! randomhousekids.com

Educators and librarians, for a variety of teaching tools, visit us at RHTeachersLibrarians.com

Library of Congress Cataloging-in-Publication Data
Names: Reynolds, Luke, author. | Mack, Jeff, illustrator.
Title: If my love were a fire truck / by Luke Reynolds ; illustrated by Jeff Mack.
Description: First edition. | New York : Doubleday, [2017] | Summary: "A rhyming celebration of the love between a father and son" —Provided by publisher.
Identifiers: LCCN 2015040154 | ISBN 978-1-101-93740-2 (trade) | ISBN 978-1-101-93741-9 (lib. bdg.) | ISBN 978-1-101-93742-6 (ebook)
Subjects: | CYAC: Stories in rhyme. | Fathers and sons—Fiction.
Classification: LCC PZ8.3.R334 If 2017 | DDC [E]—dc23

The illustrations in this book were created in mixed media.

MANUFACTURED IN CHINA
10 9 8 7 6 5 4 3 2 1
First Edition

Random House Children's Books supports the
First Amendment and celebrates the right to read.

IF MY LOVE WERE A FIRE TRUCK

A Daddy's Love Song

by Luke Reynolds

illustrated by Jeff Mack

Doubleday Books for Young Readers

Sky grows dark,
moon glows bright.

Climb in bed,
turn out the light.

It's dreamtime now.
I'll meet you there.

My love for you
goes everywhere. . . .

If my love were a fire truck,
its sirens would flash all night.

And if my love were a rocket ship,
it would blast off out of sight.

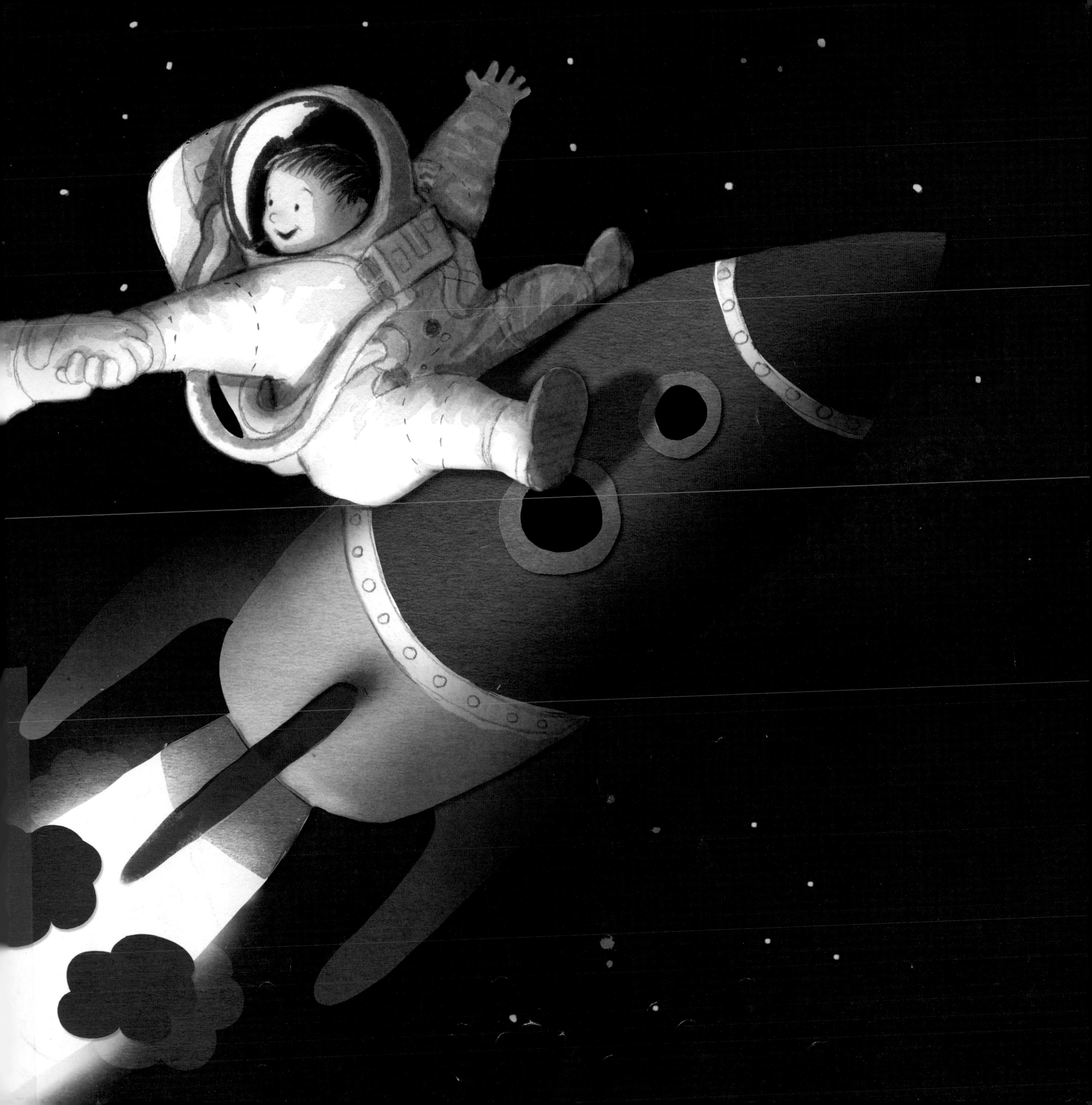

If my love were an elephant,
it would stomp from tree to tree.

And if my love were a great blue whale,
it would splash across the sea.

If my love were a marching band,
its drums would crash and boom.

And if my love were a racing car,
it would rev and rattle and *vroom*.

If my love were a rodeo horse,
it would bound and buck and bray.

And if my love were a building site,
it would clang and buzz all day.

If my love were a knight's big shield,
it would fight any dragon's flame.

And if my love were a lion's roar,
it would thunder across the plain.

If my love were a deep-sea dive,
it would touch the ocean floor.

And if my love were a surfing champ,
it would ride every wave to shore.

If my love were a firework,
it would blast long past this song.

And if my love were a big bear hug,
it would snuggle you all night long.